The Picture Stone

Note for Librarians: A cataloguing record for this book is available from Library and Archives Canada at www.collectionscanada.ca/amicus/index-e.html
ISBN 1-4120-9053-9

Printed in Victoria, BC, Canada. Printed on paper with minimum 30% recycled fibre.
Trafford's print shop runs on "green energy" from solar, wind and other environmentally-friendly power sources.

Offices in Canada, USA, Ireland and UK

Book sales for North America and international:
Trafford Publishing, 6E–2333 Government St.,
Victoria, BC V8T 4P4 CANADA
phone 250 383 6864 (toll-free 1 888 232 4444)
fax 250 383 6804; email to orders@trafford.com
Book sales in Europe:
Trafford Publishing (UK) Limited, 9 Park End Street, 2nd Floor
Oxford, UK OX1 1HH UNITED KINGDOM
phone 44 (0)1865 722 113 (local rate 0845 230 9601)
facsimile 44 (0)1865 722 868; info.uk@trafford.com
Order online at:
trafford.com/06-0809

10 9 8 7 6 5 4 3 2 1

Dedicated To

Cassandra, Jessica, Noah and Lucy
Four Delightful Grandchildren
Truly blessed with the special power

Acknowledgements

To our granddaughter Cassandra who taught us all how to play the game *"**what if**."* It was her thirst for knowledge and eagerness to read that provided the inspiration and motivation to write this story.

To my wife Kathy for her 41 years of unending support. Without her editing skills, keen eye for detail and encouragement, this project would not have been possible.

Chapter 1

To those who knew her well, Mindy Magee was the happiest child you could imagine. She had two loving parents, a great sister named Tess and a large brown floppy-eared Basset Hound, named Tippy. She was one of those children with a great sense of humour, a smile that would brighten your day and a personality to match.

Mindy and her family lived in a beautiful home near the edge of a large city. To Mindy, their house was very special because of its location. Although their home was situated in the city, their back yard overlooked a large meadow populated with many different species of plants and wildlife. Immediately behind the meadow was a small winding creek that led to a huge marsh where countless numbers of birds and animals spent the majority of their time. From Mindy's point of view, their yard represented the best of both worlds – city and country combined.

Because the birds and animals were constantly travelling back and forth between the meadow and the marsh, Mindy and Tess considered themselves extremely lucky. They were in a perfect location to monitor the daily lives of all the creatures that lived just outside their back door. Frequently, they had the opportunity to study the activities of hawks, ducks, geese, grouse and partridge. Sometimes, if they were lucky, they would see a fox hunting in the meadow or a deer making its way along the creek.

During the winter months, it seemed as if all the rabbits from the meadow moved into their back yard. Occasionally her dad would feed them and she and Tess would watch from their living room window.

Most weekends during the summer months, Mindy's family packed their car with supplies and everyone, including Tippy, would make the trip to their cottage located at a quiet lake not far away. Both Mindy and Tess loved the cottage and eagerly looked forward to their Friday trip all week long. By the time Friday finally arrived, they could hardly wait to get on their way.

To Mindy, their cottage was also a special place. From their covered front deck they had a fabulous view of the lake and it seemed as if birds were everywhere.

Even though the cottage was usually a quiet and peaceful place, there were times Mindy had reason to question exactly how quiet it really was, especially in the early morning. There was no doubt she enjoyed waking up to the sounds of singing birds, but those pesky Magpies were not what she called the peaceful singing of songbirds. Frequently she found herself wondering if Magpies ever slept. To her, it seemed as soon as there was any sign of dawn approaching, they would be at it again. She never had any idea what their usual morning fuss was about, but they seemed to go through it almost every morning. Then, for some unknown reason, once she was wide-awake they would stop fussing and fly away. It was almost as if it was their duty to wake her.

One of the most awesome things Mindy admired about their cottage was the huge number of stars that filled the night sky. In the evening their family would often sit around a crackling fire their dad would build in the fire pit next to the lake. Just as it was getting dark and the fire was turning to hot coals, they would roast marshmallows, something she and Tess especially enjoyed.

Occasionally there would be a spectacular sunset and as darkness slowly approached, it would become very calm as the crickets began to sing. Sometimes they saw a bat fly past or fireflies making their way through the tall grass and shrubs along the pathway leading to the lake. Slowly but surely, stars would begin to appear and soon the entire heavens would be filled with millions of sparkling diamonds. At times, it almost seemed as if the twinkling stars were dancing to the singing of the crickets. Mindy couldn't imagine a place more beautiful. By the time she and Tess would finally be called to their beds, the moon would be shining brightly and the northern lights dancing about in the sky. It truly was an awesome sight!

It was while at the cottage, during one of those hot lazy summer days, that Mindy began her incredible adventure. She had just finished her lunch and was feeling a little sleepy. Instead of taking a nap, she decided to sit under a nice shade tree near the cottage. She selected a couple of her favorite books, picked up her small red chair and made her way to a nice shady spot not too far from the lake where she could still hear the water lapping against the stones. She sat there for a few minutes looking through her books, but her eyes soon became a little drowsy. The next thing she knew they were closed. She wasn't asleep, but it sure felt good to close them for a moment or two – just to rest them.

Chapter 2

Moments later, Mindy was startled by a small gust of wind somewhere next to her body. She quickly opened her eyes and there in front of her sat the most beautiful golden bird she'd ever seen. In fact, she'd never seen such a large bird in her entire life. At first glance, it frightened her and her immediate response was to spring to her feet and run away. Just as she rose from the chair, the bird cocked its head to one side, looked directly at her and said, "Hi Mindy, how are you today?"

To say the least, Mindy was shocked! A

talking bird! It was unbelievable! The only type of bird Mindy was aware of that could talk was a parrot, but this bird was much larger and looked nothing like a parrot. She really didn't know what to think. She looked at the bird hoping to confirm it was a parrot, but it sure didn't look like any type of parrot she'd ever seen. It was much too large and it was a solid gold color. Mindy didn't know a lot about birds, but she knew enough to realize the bird in front of her was definitely not a parrot.

There was little doubt Mindy was frightened by the encounter. She could feel her heart pounding in her chest and knew she should get away from the bird as quickly as possible. Even though she knew what she should do, something told her the bird wasn't going to harm her.

Mindy slowly began backing away to place some distance between the bird and herself. As she inched backwards, she avoided direct eye contact with the bird and in a faint little voice managed to say, "Pardon me?"

The bird immediately hopped toward her and in a clear voice again greeted her. "Hi Mindy, how are you today?"

This time Mindy looked straight into the eyes of the bird and in a clear stern voice said. "Excuse me, but how do you know my name, and what kind of a bird are you anyway?"

The bird cocked its head to one side and replied. "Well Mindy, it's a long story. I'm known as a Gruck and I flew here from the land of Zot. It took me a long time to get here and forever to find you. Did you know you're a hard person to track down?"

Mindy was shocked! First a talking bird called a Gruck and on top of that, it knew her name! Surely this must be a dream. She pinched herself, thinking it might be a dream. It really hurt. "This can't be a dream," she said to herself. "I've never heard of anything like this before. I've seen lots of birds, but never one like this. My dad and grandpa know a lot about birds, but no one ever mentioned anything about a Gruck, much less one that talks."

Mindy looked at the bird in disbelief. "I

don't believe you're real. Is this some sort of trick?"

"No!" replied the bird. "I really am a Gruck, just as a duck is a duck and a goose is a goose and so on. My name is Bolo. Princess Min from the land of Zot sent me to find and invite you to a party at the palace next Saturday afternoon at two o'clock. Do you think you could come to the party?"

Mindy couldn't believe her ears. "I'm sorry," she replied politely. "I don't know who you are. I've never heard of Princess Min or the land of Zot."

"Don't worry," explained Bolo. "The land of Zot is a beautiful place you will really like. Princess Min is a girl about your age and she would really like to play with you. If your mom and dad will let you attend the party, I'll escort you to the castle next Saturday and make sure you get home safely. You don't need to worry because it's my job to look after you."

Mindy stared at the bird for what seemed the longest time. All the while she was trying to decide if what she was seeing was some sort of elaborate practical joke. As it turned out, she did have reason to suspect a practical joke. To her family and friends Mindy was well known as a practical joker so she had reason to suspect someone might be attempting to even the score. On the other hand though, she couldn't visualize how anyone could construct such an elaborate joke. "Who is Princess Min?" she asked.

"Well," replied Bolo, "Princess Min is the Queen's daughter."

"What Queen?" asked Mindy.

"The Queen of Zot," he replied. "To make a long story short, Princess Min doesn't have very many friends because she lives in a large castle. She heard about you from some of the other birds from Zot that have seen you at your cottage this summer. She really wants to meet you, so I was asked to find you and invite you to the party. She would be so happy if you could attend. I would be very pleased if I could return and tell her you will be coming to the party. Will you please attend?"

Mindy thought about Bolo's request for a moment or two before she replied. She wasn't sure if she should accept the invitation but in the end nodded her head in agreement.

"Well I suppose I could, if my Mom and Dad will let me."

Bolo looked very pleased as he settled into a comfortable position beside her chair. "Well, go ask them and I'll wait for you here."

Chapter 3

Mindy skipped to the cottage and looked for her mom. Her mother and grandma were sitting on the covered front deck of the cottage where they were quietly talking as they watched the sailboats on the lake.

"Mom," asked Mindy, "is it okay if I go to a party at Princess Min's castle next Saturday afternoon?"

Mindy's mother looked at her for the longest time before she replied. "Who on earth is Princess Min?"

"Well," explained Mindy, "Princess Min is

about my age and she lives in the castle in the land of Zot. She's having a party next Saturday at two o'clock and I'm invited."

"Who invited you?" asked her mother.

"Bolo did," she replied.

Mindy's mother stared at her with a blank expression on her face. She paused for what seemed an eternity and then with a raised eyebrow asked. "What on earth are you talking about child?"

Mindy took a deep breath. She knew it was a complicated story, but she did her very best to outline the circumstances as to how she came to be invited to the party. Being as brief as possible, she carefully told her mother and grandma the whole story about Bolo and how he came from the land of Zot, just to invite her to Princess Min's party. She even suggested they come into the yard with her and talk to Bolo themselves, but her grandma and mom seemed a bit too comfortable to get up and follow her.

After she finished the story, Mindy's mother looked at her, smiled at grandma and said. "Well, I guess you can go if you want. You can do anything you want in the land of make believe."

"But this isn't make believe," Mindy insisted. "Come and talk to Bolo yourself," she pleaded.

"Sure child, sure child," replied her mom. "It's okay, we'll take your word for it."

Mindy's mom looked at Grandma and winked. They both smiled. What Mindy didn't realize was that both her mom and grandma thought she'd just made up the story about Bolo and Princess Min. They thought she was playing.

Mindy dashed back to the tree in the yard where she found Bolo sleeping comfortably beside the chair. As soon as she sat down, Bolo slowly opened one eye, looked at her, cocked his head to one side and said, "Well?"

"My mom says I can go," reported Mindy.

"Great," Bolo replied. "I'll come for you next Saturday just after lunch. Come to the same place, and wait for me."

"Okay," said Mindy, "but how will you

take me there and how far away is the land of Zot?"

"Don't fret," Bolo replied in a reassuring voice. "Details, details, details! It's my job to look after you, so let me worry about the details."

"Okay," said Mindy. "See you on Saturday."

And with that, the marvellous golden bird slowly rose from the ground without moving its wings or making any noise whatsoever. It continued to rise toward the treetops at which point it looked down and said, "See you Mindy." Then, as suddenly as it had appeared, it vanished into thin air. Mindy didn't see it fly away – it simply disappeared.

Mindy sat there for the longest time trying to understand what she'd just witnessed. Nothing like this had ever happened to her before. Was it real, or was her imagination just playing tricks on her? After thinking about it for a long time, she decided it must have been real. "That's it," she sternly said to herself.

"I'm going to the party and see what this is all about."

With her final decision behind her, she tucked her books under her arm, picked up her chair and went inside the cottage for a drink of water. Out on the front deck her mom and grandma were still sitting, just enjoying the beautiful day.

"Done playing?" asked her mother.

"I wasn't playing," she insisted. "I was talking to Bolo."

"Sure," replied her mom. "What do you say we go to the beach for a swim when Tess wakes up from her nap?"

"Great plan," agreed Mindy.

A few minutes later Tess was up and ready to go. They packed their beach toys and left for the beach. For the remainder of the afternoon they played in the sand, swam in the water and even had ice cream treats. It was truly a wonderful day.

No matter how hard she tried though, Mindy was unable to get her mind off the strange encounter with the bird. Each time she thought about it, the more she always ended up asking herself the same question. "What really happened?"

When they got back from the beach, she rushed into the cottage and told her dad and grandpa about Bolo's invitation. They both listened very carefully as she told them the whole story. Her dad asked a lot of questions about the great golden bird, but both he and grandpa couldn't seem to determine exactly what kind of bird she'd seen. Grandpa asked her if she was sure she hadn't just fallen asleep and had a little dream, but Mindy insisted she'd seen a beautiful golden bird that talked to her.

After some time, the adults stopped asking question, but Mindy could see them smiling to themselves and she soon got the feeling they didn't believe her. She was a little annoyed the adults didn't believe her, but in the end it made her even more determined.

"I'll show them," she said to herself. "When I go to the party next week, I'll take my mom's camera with me and bring back some evidence to prove I'm right."

That evening, as they sat around the campfire, Mindy looked up and carefully scanned the sky. The stars were beginning to appear and before long the heavens were filled with tiny pinpoints of light. As she studied the stars, she noticed they seemed to sparkle more brightly than usual and she was certain the crickets were much more active than the last time she'd been at the cottage.

The night soon became very still and far off in the distance she heard the distinct calls of some night birds. She listened to their mournful calls and found herself wondering if maybe they were Grucks or some of the other birds from the land of Zot.

Later, as she crawled into bed, she found herself going over the events of the day once again. She thought about Bolo, the land of Zot and Princess Min. What was it all about? She knew none of the adults really believed she actually met a talking bird, but she also knew what she'd experienced was very real. After all, she'd pinched herself just to make sure it wasn't a dream.

As she lay there wondering about the land of Zot, she closed her eyes and tried to picture it. Slowly but surely, she drifted off into the wonderful world called dreamland.

A Day at the Beach

Chapter 4

The following week seemed to drag on forever. Every single morning after she woke up, Mindy would look across the meadow behind their house to see if she could identify all the different species of birds that lived there. No matter how hard she studied them, she never saw a bird anything like Bolo. All of the birds in the meadow were much smaller and not a single one had gold colored feathers. Even though she tried to convince herself the bird she'd met was a very rare species, she still couldn't help but wonder if Bolo was real, or if she'd just imagined him.

By Wednesday, she was becoming a little discouraged. Her Dad told them he wasn't sure if they could make it to the cottage on the weekend because he had to travel out of town to work and might not return until very late Friday night. Then, to make matters worse, on Thursday it began to rain. It rained most of the day and was still raining when she went to bed on Thursday night.

When Mindy awoke on Friday morning, it was still raining. She was sure there would be no trip to the cottage this weekend. As she played with Tess, she looked out their living room window every few minutes, only to see the raindrops slowly sliding down the windowpane. She even listened to the weather report on the radio. The radio announcer said the rain should stop by noon, but from looking outside her window, all Mindy could see was dark clouds and more rain. She felt very sad.

To everyone's surprise, the rain suddenly stopped shortly after lunch and the sun began to peek out from behind the clouds. It was as if someone had uttered a few magic words and "Presto," the rain stopped. A few minutes later, she saw a small patch of blue sky and almost immediately her dad was home from work. His plans had been changed because of the rain so he decided to come home early. Before she knew it, they were packed and on their way to the cottage.

That evening as she watched the sun setting across the lake, Mindy sat on the front steps of the cottage and wondered what tomorrow would bring. Once again she looked up at the stars and wondered if the land of Zot was up there. She wasn't sure what to think, but she knew tomorrow all her questions would be answered. With those thoughts on her mind, she went to her room and crawled into bed. As she lay there in the dark, all she could hear was the soothing sound of crickets as they chirped just outside her bedroom window. She lay there thinking about Bolo and was soon fast asleep.

Chapter 5

Once again, Mindy was rudely awakened by the annoying sound of Magpies in the trees just outside her bedroom window. She opened her eyes and was surprised to find it was daylight. She couldn't believe it was morning already. It seemed as if she'd just fallen asleep a few minutes ago. She quietly slipped out of bed and made her way to the window and looked outside. It was still a bit cloudy and judging from the water on the picnic table it had obviously rained sometime during the night. She studied the sky for a moment or two and concluded the clouds would soon disappear. "It should be a grand day for a party," she said to herself.

Before long, everyone was up and breakfast was soon on the table. Although there was no hurry, Mindy rushed through her breakfast and eagerly made her way outside to the tree where she'd seen the golden bird. She carefully scanned all the nearby trees and shrubs hoping she might get a glimpse of it somewhere. In spite of her efforts though, it was just as she suspected. The bird was nowhere to be seen. It wasn't as if she really expected to see it, because it was still too early in the day, but she thought the area should be checked anyway – just in case.

Mindy spent the remainder of the morning playing with Tess in the area around the cottage. Although their activities kept them both occupied, the more she wished for time to hurry, the slower it seemed to pass. She was beginning to learn the pitfalls of watching the clock.

Every so often she would abandon Tess, go

back to the tree and scan the area for any signs of Bolo. After what seemed an eternity, her mother finally called them for lunch and she knew it would soon be time to go to the party. To say the least she was very excited, but then again, she still had those lingering doubts in her mind. It always came down to the same old question. Was Bolo real or had she just imagined him?

As soon as lunch was finished, Mindy formally announced to the family she was going to her room to prepare for the party. Everyone looked a little surprised and wanted to know what party she was talking about.

"Princess Min's party," she replied.

"Oh right," said her mom, "I totally forgot about that."

Mindy's grandpa smiled at her across the table as he looked over his reading glasses. "This time," he instructed, "make sure you get us a couple of those fancy golden feathers you told us about. Maybe then we can figure out exactly what kind of bird you saw."

Mindy nodded her head in response to

grandpa's suggestion, but she didn't reply. She just politely excused herself from the table and went straight to her room.

Once again, Mindy was mindful of the fact that all the adults were looking at each other and smiling amongst themselves. She knew they found the situation amusing, but in her eyes it was because they just didn't understand what had taken place the week before.

In spite of everything, she resolved not to let their amusement bother her. After all, she was the one who saw the bird and she knew it was up to her to prove her point. As best she could, she erased all the negative thoughts from her mind, picked up her favorite book and made her way to the tree where she'd first met Bolo. She knew the truth would soon be known.

Chapter 6

Waiting for something is never a comfortable task. Time always moves along like a snail and it's especially tiresome, not to mention disappointing, if what you're waiting for never occurs. Mindy had often heard the adults in her life use the expression ***"hurry up and wait,"*** as they described the fast pace of their lives. It was only lately though, that she'd come to understand exactly what ***"hurry up and wait,"*** really meant.

For certain, she was no longer a stranger to the waiting game. She'd just spent an entire week waiting and wondering. Coupled with the boredom of having to wait and wonder for a whole week, she'd also been wrestling with the distinct possibility that in the end what she was waiting for might never occur.

This time the wait proved to be no different. More than fifteen minutes had already passed and Bolo was still nowhere to be seen. As much as she wanted to believe he would keep his appointment, she once again found those little doubts–as to whether or not Bolo was real–creeping back into her mind. She tried desperately to erase all the negative thoughts, but try as she might it was absolutely impossible. To make matters worse, she began to think how amused the adults would be if she had to admit she'd only imagined Bolo. In desperation, she looked up in the sky, across the lake and even into the forest, but there was no sign of Bolo anywhere. Feeling a little discouraged, she sat down on the ground beneath the tree.

"Maybe if I close my eyes like last time," she said to herself, "Bolo will find me."

Almost instantly her prayers were answered. She had just closed her eyes for a few seconds when she felt something move behind her. She immediately stood up and there behind her stood a huge bird. At first she didn't know exactly what to say or do. The bird looked a lot like Bolo, but wasn't quite the same. Its feathers were gold in color, but it also had some large red spots on its body.

Mindy looked carefully at the bird. "Bolo?" she asked.

"Yes," replied the bird.

"What happened to you?"

"Well, Princess Min and I were playing this morning and she accidentally sprayed me with some red paint which left me with a few red patches on my feathers."

Mindy smiled a little. "You sure look funny."

"I know," Bolo replied, "but it really isn't very funny because it makes it much more difficult for me to fly. As a result, you'll have to use the magic stick to get to Princess Min's."

"What magic stick?" asked Mindy.

"This one," he replied, as he stretched out one of his gigantic wings. Tucked under his wing was an odd looking twisted and bent stick. The stick was almost as long as Mindy was tall. "Here, take the stick," he instructed.

Mindy placed her book on the ground, took the stick from under his wing and held it in her hand. To Mindy, the stick looked just like any old ordinary branch from a dead tree. As she looked a little closer though, she noticed it appeared to be different colors, depending which way she moved it. "Is this really a magic stick?" she asked.

"Absolutely," he replied. "It's called a rainbow stick. When you wave it properly and say the magic words a small rainbow will appear. Listen very carefully to my instructions and do exactly as I tell you."

"First," he went on, "hold the stick in your right hand."

Mindy placed the stick in her right hand and awaited further instructions.

"Now raise the end of the stick above your head and repeat these words."

"Bzing! Bzang! Bezot!"
"Take us now to the land of Zot!"

Mindy didn't really believe anything would happen, but she decided to give it a try anyway. She slowly raised the stick above her head and repeated the magic words.

Almost immediately, a fine mist filled the air. Directly above her head appeared the most beautiful rainbow she'd ever seen. It was not a large rainbow, but it was directly over her head, just like a large archway. Mindy realized she was standing under the archway of the rainbow. When she looked behind her, she could see the cottage. When she looked through the misty archway, she could see a narrow winding cobblestone path in the middle of a large meadow filled with beautiful flowers and colorful birds. As the mist slowly cleared, she saw the sky over the meadow was a very deep blue color and off in the distance next to some large hills, she could see what looked like a huge castle. Mindy just stood there. She couldn't believe her eyes. This truly was a magic stick!

After a moment or two, Bolo hopped up beside her. "Okay Mindy, hold the stick above your head and walk toward the cobblestone path."

Mindy didn't even think about it. For some reason, she did exactly as he instructed. When their feet touched the cobblestone path, the rainbow instantly disappeared. They were both left standing on the path in the middle of the meadow.

Mindy wasn't sure exactly what had happened, but wherever they were it was a beautiful day. Seconds earlier, she'd been standing by a tree near their cottage and it had been quite windy. In the meadow where she now stood, there was absolutely no wind at all. She quickly looked to her left and right and was instantly struck by the sheer beauty of her surroundings.

Everywhere she looked there were countless wildflowers and small shrubs in full bloom. Looking up toward the sky, she saw large numbers of brightly colored birds as they flew about. If only her dad and mom could see these birds she thought. She was sure they had never seen birds like these before. Far off in the distance she could see what appeared to be a huge castle. She was mystified. Yes, there was no doubt about it. Something truly magical had taken place right before her eyes!

Once the shock of everything began to subside, Mindy looked back toward where the cottage had been. No matter where she looked, the cottage was nowhere in sight. Instinctively, she started to panic, but Bolo did his best to comfort and assure her everything would be fine.

"Don't worry Mindy," he said. "There's nothing to fear. Just think positive. You're going to have a great time at Princess Min's party. I promise you I'll get you home safe and sound as soon as the party is over."

"But how will I get back?" she asked.

"With the rainbow stick," he replied. "The rainbow stick brought you here and it will take you home too. It's one of the magical methods of travel between our land and yours so don't worry about getting home. We better not waste any more time. Princess Min has been waiting a long time to meet you so we'd best be on our way."

"Okay," said Mindy. "I'm ready." She took one last look toward where the cottage had been and they both started down the path toward the castle.

Chapter 7

Walking together along the path, Bolo told Mindy all about the land of Zot. "The land of Zot," he explained, "is a magical place where nothing bad ever happens. It's a place of true beauty and magic. In the land of Zot even the animals can talk to everyone. Whenever we have problems we just sit down and talk about them and in no time at all everything gets resolved."

What a marvellous place thought Mindy. The more she thought about it, the more she couldn't help but think what it would be like if she could talk to her dog. Many times Tippy would stand in front of her wagging his tail. The problem was, she never had any idea what he wanted. Usually it ended up with her taking him for a walk, but she never knew for certain if that's what he really wanted in the first place.

Soon, they came to a small wooden foot-bridge crossing a peaceful brook that wound through the meadow. Mindy paused at the bridge and looked down into the water. Beneath the bridge she saw a large colorful fish that Bolo identified as a rainbow fish. As she looked further along the banks of the brook, she spied a huge frog sitting on a large lily pad. It was the largest bullfrog she'd ever seen. As she stood there attempting to estimate its size, the frog suddenly cleared its throat with a "chug-a-rum" and in a raspy voice said, "Hi Mindy, it's good to see you."

Mindy looked at Bolo in disbelief. "I don't believe this. First a talking bird and now a frog!"

"Sure," explained Bolo. "As I told you

before, all the animals here can talk to you. I told everyone you were coming to Princess Min's party so everyone knows about you. You're our special guest."

Mindy didn't know what to think, but she felt good knowing she was considered their special guest.

It was about then Mindy suddenly realized she'd forgotten to bring her mother's camera. "Oh drats," she moaned. "I forgot the camera."

"That's okay," Bolo assured her. "Don't worry, we can easily fix that problem. We'll get you a picture stone instead."

"A picture stone?" asked Mindy.

"Yes," he explained. "Cameras don't work very well here anyway, so we'll just find you a nice picture stone. You'll see, it's much better than any camera."

"But I need to take something back with me."

"I know," he replied. "That's why we need to find you a picture stone. Let's walk beside the brook and see if we can find something suitable."

Mindy accepted his offer and they both climbed down the bank toward the brook and slowly walked along the edge looking for the perfect stone.

"Don't worry Mindy," said Bolo. "When you find a special stone it will be much better than any camera, just you wait and see."

After walking a short distance, they came upon a rocky area filled with a large variety of brightly colored stones of many different shapes and sizes. Bolo encouraged her to take her time in selecting a stone. He told her to choose a color she liked and then look for one of the right size.

"Make sure it's not too big," he instructed. "You'll have to carry it, so don't pick one that's too heavy."

Bolo was unaware that Mindy was an expert in the art of selecting stones. To her friends, Mindy was well known as a serious rock hound. At the cottage she'd spent many hours searching for perfect specimens to add to her rock collection and by any standard, her collection was considered very substantial. She'd been rock collecting for as long as she could remember and had specimens of every size, shape and composition you could possibly imagine. Mindy was so avid about her rock collecting that as far as her family was concerned, she was their "family geologist."

Mindy knew the stone she was about to select would be her most prized possession. As a result, she began the detailed process of carefully examining stones of the proper size and shape. Some time later, she noticed a beautiful brilliant green flat stone about the size of a large coin. It stood out from the other stones around it and seemed about the right size. She carefully reached down and picked it up.

"Excellent choice!" exclaimed Bolo. "You've selected a Moss stone. It will make a perfect picture stone."

Mindy carefully cleaned and polished the stone in her hand, but it wasn't until the stone was fully cleaned that its true characteristics were revealed. Without a doubt she'd never encountered a specimen that was so smooth and shiny. When she held it up to the light and carefully examined its surface, it was so shiny she could see her face. It reminded her of a small mirror.

"What a wonderful find," she said to herself. "This will be my prized possession."

Bolo looked very pleased as he gave her further instructions. "Hold the stone tightly in your left hand and follow me."

Mindy held the stone in her hand as he instructed and followed him back onto the cobblestone path. After walking a short distance, he stepped off the path and hopped over to a large purple flower growing beside the path. He told her to touch the flower with the stone and then close her eyes.

Mindy followed his instructions exactly. A moment or two later, he instructed her to open her eyes. She opened them and looked at the stone, but it didn't seem any different than before. In spite of her doubts, Bolo assured her the stone really did have magical powers.

"Whenever you want to picture the land of

Zot," he explained, "just hold the stone in your left hand and close your eyes. Give it a try."

Mindy placed the stone in her left hand and closed her eyes. What she saw was spectacular! It was as if a whole album of pictures were in front of her. She was able to go through the pictures of every single thing she'd seen since she arrived in the land of Zot. When she opened her eyes, Bolo asked her if she liked what she saw. "Cool!" she exclaimed. "It was just like watching a movie!"

"Keep the stone with you at all times," instructed Bolo, "and you will always be able to see pictures of where you have been no matter where you go. This is your special stone and it will only work for you. Now, we'd better be on our way or we'll be late for the party."

Chapter 8

Bolo and Mindy continued along the path talking about the beautiful flowers and birds as they walked. He told her the names of all the birds and flowers they saw, but there were so many she couldn't possibly remember them all.

Soon, they came upon a large stone fence that had a stone bench built into it. Bolo suggested Mindy sit down for a little rest, so she climbed onto the bench and sat down.

"I'm sorry for making you walk so far Mindy," he explained, "but because of the paint on my feathers, I can't fly and carry you too. If we just wait here a short while, I'm sure the Queen's carriage will soon arrive and you can ride to the castle in style."

Sitting there on the stone bench, Mindy had a good opportunity to look around. The sky was a clear deep blue color. The grass of the meadow was dark green and as far as the eye could see, there were small patches of different varieties of wild flowers in full bloom. They were the most beautiful flowers she'd ever seen. Scattered about were small shrubs and trees. From where she sat she could see the birds flying from tree to tree and the bees busily moving from flower to flower across the meadow. It was such a peaceful place.

After a short time, Mindy spied what looked like a horse and carriage off in the distance. It was hard to make out all the details, but the carriage appeared to be headed toward them.

"Here comes your escort," announced Bolo. "When they get here, you can ride in the carriage and I'll fly back to the castle on my own."

"Can't we just walk?" asked Mindy.

"Well, we could," he replied, "but there's still a long way to go. See the big hill off in the distance?"

"Yes," replied Mindy.

"Well, the castle is just at the edge of the valley right by the hill. You can't see it from here, but it's quite visible once you travel around the side of the hill. The hill is about one mile away so it would be better if you rode in the carriage."

"But I'm afraid of horses," said Mindy rather timidly.

"Don't worry," Bolo assured her, "the horse is very gentle and it would never harm you."

A few moments later the carriage arrived. Mindy just sat in complete awe. The carriage was shiny black with bright red wheels. There were silver ornaments all over the carriage and it was pulled by a beautiful white horse wearing a shiny black leather harness decorated with gold and silver fasteners. The horse had a black patch on its forehead and perfect black hooves. Its tail and mane were braided and decorated with beautiful gold rings.

On the driver's seat of the carriage sat a rather small man wearing a white suit and bright red top hat with matching leather gloves. Seated in the rear seat of the carriage was a young girl, about Mindy's age and size.

On closer inspection, Mindy came to realize the girl sitting in the carriage was not only her size, but looked a lot like her as well. In fact, if she didn't know better, she would have thought they were twins.

The instant the horse came to a stop, the little girl sprang from the carriage and ran over to where Mindy was sitting. Before Mindy could say or do anything, the girl gave her a big hug.

"Thank you, thank you, thank you, for coming to my party," she said excitedly. "I'm Princess Min and I'm so glad to meet you. Everything is arranged at the castle and we're going to have a wonderful time."

Mindy was so surprised she couldn't speak for a moment or two. When she finally calmed down, she looked at Princess Min and exclaimed, "I can't believe how much we look alike!"

"I know," said Princess Min. "I've known about you for a long time and I'm so happy we've finally met. I can hardly wait for us to get back to the castle. We're going to have a great time."

From that point on, Mindy and Princess Min were like two long lost twins. It was as if they had known each other all their lives. They climbed up into the carriage and as they started toward the castle Mindy looked behind just in time to give Bolo a wave as he rose into the air and flew overhead in the direction of the castle.

During their journey toward the castle, Princess Min told Mindy a little about the party. "There will be many other children at the party," she said, "but you are my special guest and I know you'll have a wonderful time. We're even going to have a magician come to entertain us. I can hardly wait."

Mindy tried to picture a magician in a land of magic, but she couldn't. "You know Min, it seems to me everything here is magic, so what kind of special power does the magician have?" she asked.

Princess Min laughed and said, "I can't tell you. You'll just have to wait and see. The only thing I can tell you is, it's going to be the greatest performance we've ever seen."

As the carriage slowly rumbled along the path, Princess Min reached into her pocket and removed a piece of string constructed of threads of many different colors. "Here," she said, "hold out your right arm." Mindy held out her right arm and Princess Min carefully tied the string around her right wrist.

"What is it?" asked Mindy.

"It's a rainbow bracelet," Princess Min replied. "It's a special bracelet you need to wear so you can talk to all the children who will be at the party."

"I don't understand," said Mindy.

"Well," explained Princess Min, "the children coming to the party are from all over the world and they all speak different languages. By wearing the rainbow bracelet, everyone will be able to understand each other."

Mindy didn't ask any more questions. She already knew the land of Zot was a magical place and she knew this was just one more thing considered normal for the people of Zot. At times, she thought for sure she must be in the middle of a dream. If it was a dream though, it was an incredible one and she knew she didn't want it to end. In her left pocket was her picture stone and on her right wrist was a rainbow bracelet. Sitting there in the carriage with Princess Min, talking and enjoying the beautiful scenery, she couldn't help but wonder what would be next.

Chapter 9

Slowly but surely, the carriage came closer and closer to the large hill Bolo had pointed out earlier. As they made their way around a curve in the road, they entered a shady forest area with huge trees on both sides of the road. After traveling a short distance, the forest suddenly ended and there before them was a beautiful bright green lawn trimmed so short it looked like velvet. On the opposite side of the lawn was a huge stone castle surrounded by flowerbeds filled with bright red flowers.

From the top of the castle flew three bright red flags.

Mindy was speechless. The castle was so large she had trouble believing it was real. Princess Min talked on and on, but Mindy hardly heard a word because she was too busy studying everything around her. All she could think about was what awaited her at the castle and the wonderful story she'd have to tell when she returned home.

Before she realized it, the carriage arrived at the castle and they were outside the main entrance. The instant the carriage came to a stop, Princess Min grabbed Mindy by the hand and together they jumped down from the carriage and hurried to the large doors at the front of the castle. The moment they arrived at the castle's front entrance, the huge doors slowly swung open and a smartly dressed doorman greeted them. Within seconds they were through the door and standing at the foot of a grand ornate staircase leading to a large balcony on the second floor.

Hanging from the ceiling above the staircase was a huge crystal chandelier that sparkled from the sunlight shining on it through windows above the front doors. Princess Min immediately started up the stairs. Turning to Mindy, she said, "let's go up to my room. We can play up there until the other guests arrive."

Princess Min's room was breathtaking. It was located on the rear side of the castle and had two huge windows with wide sills. Each windowsill was filled with dolls and teddy bears of every type one could imagine. The bedroom floor was covered with a bright floral patterned carpet and in the centre of the room stood a huge poster bed draped with a bright red silk canopy.

From the windows of Princess Min's bedroom, Mindy had a wonderful view of the castle's huge back yard and the snow capped mountains off in the distance. The back yard was just as large as the front, but there were more gardens and hedges with fountains and stone patios. There seemed to be walkways everywhere and here and there she could see small fishponds and blooming shrubs.

Mindy leaned over the windowsill to get a better view. Off to her left, she could see several workers scurrying about setting up tables and chairs in a nice shady area of the yard. "How many will be at the party?" she asked.

"I don't know for sure," replied Princess Min, "but there will be quite a few."

Mindy had a thousand questions to ask, but there was so much to see she couldn't decide whether to ask questions, or just absorb everything that surrounded her. They talked, they played with the dolls and before they knew it, they could hear the sound of approaching horses.

Both girls rushed to the windows to see what was happening. Off in the distance they could see several carriages headed directly toward the castle. "They're coming!" exclaimed Princess Min. "Let's go and welcome them!" She grabbed Mindy by the hand and they both raced out of the room, down the grand staircase and out the rear entrance of the castle into the shaded area of the back yard.

Before long, the carriages began to arrive one by one. Each carriage was similar to the one Mindy had traveled in and each carried four children. There were children from every country of the world and as each carriage arrived, Princess Min formally greeted them.

Although Mindy desperately tried to remember where each child was from, it was much more than she could manage. She only knew one thing for certain. Regardless of which language each of them spoke, they were all able to understand each other perfectly because they were all wearing a rainbow bracelet. What a wonderful thing she thought. If only there were rainbow bracelets in her world.

Chapter 10

The party was almost a complete blur. The children laughed and played together. There were games of tag, hide and seek, musical chairs and so forth. At one point, an elephant arrived in the yard and the children took turns going for rides around the grounds.

No matter how many trips they made to the large tables for treats, the trays were always filled with hamburgers, hotdogs, cookies, cakes and ice cream. Several times, Mindy found herself just standing and looking at all the children having such fun together. It was comforting to see everyone so happy.

After they were tired from playing tag and musical chairs, Princess Min stood on a chair and in a loud formal voice shouted, "May I have your attention please!"

Almost immediately everyone stopped what they were doing and looked toward her.

"As you know," she continued, "I promised you we'd have some special entertainment today. So, without further ado, I would like to introduce you to my special friend Pedro. Pedro has magical powers and today he has agreed to entertain us with some of his magic."

The children began to clap and cheer as a beautiful black horse came trotting around the side of the castle toward them. Seated in the saddle was a tall slim man dressed like a clown. He had long blue hair, a big red nose and his face was painted red and white. He was so thin, it almost seemed he would disappear if he turned sideways. He slowly rode his horse toward the children and came to a stop next to a large table. Then, to the delight of everyone he dismounted from his horse directly onto the table. The horse bowed gracefully toward him and trotted off into the yard.

Looking rather confused, Pedro began to speak. "It's such a beautiful day today and I'm so happy to be here. Everyone is having so much fun, I wish I was a child again."

He had no sooner uttered the words when, suddenly, he began to shrink. As he stood there he got shorter and shorter, smaller and smaller. In no time at all, he was the same size as they were.

"Oh my," he said. "I guess I should be more careful. Perhaps I should have wished I was a giant."

Well, almost in an instant, he became taller and taller, bigger and bigger. He got so huge the table began to bend. Luckily he stepped off of it before it broke.

The children all began to laugh and before you knew it, they were all laughing so hard they could barely speak. Pedro looked a little confused, but he went on as if he was still not certain what to do.

"Wow, look how big I am," he said. "I think I should lose a little weight."

With that, he began to shrink until he appeared rather ordinary in size.

"Okay children, would you like to play a special game?"

"Yes, yes," they cried.

"Do any of you know how to play the game ***what if***?" he asked.

Without even thinking about it, Mindy immediately shouted, "I do, I do!"

"Well okay my dear, you go first," said Pedro.

Mindy thought for a moment and then asked, "What if you had long floppy ears like a dog?"

Pedro smiled, waved his hand and in an instant his ears turned to long floppy dog-ears. Everyone laughed and then someone shouted.

"What if you had a tail like a dog?"

Again Pedro waved his arm and almost immediately he had a long dog tail he slowly wagged back and forth.

By then, everyone was getting into the

game. Mindy laughed so hard the tears were running down her cheeks. As the game went on, Pedro changed from dog to cat, to elephant and so on. Anything you could imagine, he became.

All of sudden, Pedro shouted, "What if all of you had long floppy dog ears?"

He waved his arm and in an instant, they all had long floppy dog-ears. It was hilarious! The children began to call out different possibilities and each time Pedro waved his arm they changed from dog-ears to dog-noses, to cat-tails, and little children with elephant trunks and so on. They were having the time of their lives!

Soon, to the surprise of everyone, Pedro jumped back onto the table. A sudden hush fell over the children as they all waited in anticipation of what he would do next. Pedro paused for a brief moment as if studying the crowd. Then in a more serious voice he began to speak.

"Today, you have seen many magical things, things you will probably never see again. I'm sure you think of me as having magical powers, but you must remember you're in the land of Zot and all things are possible in the land of Zot. The reason each and every one of you is here today is because you too have a special power. Can any of you tell me what that power is?"

The children looked at one another and talked amongst themselves, but none of them could supply Pedro with an answer to his question. After all, they just thought of themselves as being ordinary. None of them could think of any special power they had. They couldn't perform magic, or do anything like they had seen in the land of Zot.

"Think about it," said Pedro. "When we were playing ***what if*** a short time ago, what made you think of the ideas to give me dog-ears and a dog tail?" Instantly, the children knew the answer.

"Our imagination," they shouted.

"You're right," said Pedro. "You were using your imagination. Without a doubt, the power of imagination is one of the most important gifts anyone can have. Many of us don't realize it, but we are all born with the power of imagination. The problem is, as we grow older we tend to forget we have the special power, much less use it to our advantage. All of you are here today because you have used your special power."

"Can you picture what it would be like if no one had the power of imagination?" he asked. "There would probably be no art or music and most of the things you use in your everyday life wouldn't exist. Every material thing you see around you in your world started with someone wondering – ***what if***? When you go home, remember, each of you have the special gift of imagination, you only have to use it."

Mindy thought about Pedro's words. She always knew she'd been gifted with a great imagination, but never before had she been aware of the power of the gift and importance of using it wisely.

And so it was, standing there beside children from every country of the world that

Mindy Magee made a pact with herself vowing she would never forget the power of her gift and what it could achieve.

While the children stood about talking, Pedro began to speak again. "Well children, "I'm afraid the time has come when we must all make our way home. Princess Min has asked me to help get everyone safely home so I would like you to join hands and form a large circle."

The children immediately began to join hands and started forming a large circle in the middle of the yard. As they were forming the circle, the black horse trotted over to the table where Pedro was standing. In one swift movement, Pedro was once again seated in the saddle. This time he no longer looked thin and tall. He looked very ordinary except for his clown suit. Slowly, Pedro and his horse made their way to the middle of the circle where they were soon completely surrounded by children holding hands.

As time went on, the circle grew to be very large and for the first time Mindy began to understand how many different languages were spoken throughout the world. She also came to realize that no matter how different the children seemed they were really very much alike. Not only did they enjoy playing the same games, they all laughed the same way, played the same way and most importantly, they were all blessed with the wonderful gift of imagination.

"Now," said Pedro, "say goodbye to each other and shortly we'll be on our way."

Mindy wasn't sure what would happen next. She said goodbye to the children around her and looked up to see Princess Min slowly walking toward her. As Princess Min came closer and closer, Mindy began to feel a little sad. On one hand she was eager to go home and tell her family of her adventure, but on the other she was having such a great time with Princess Min she didn't want to leave.

Princess Min threw her arms around Mindy and gave her a hug. "Don't worry, we'll meet again someday," she said. "Just remember, every time we look at ourselves in the mirror, we'll think of each other."

Mindy had no sooner finished saying her farewell to Princess Min when Bolo landed on the grass behind her. He waddled toward her and he too, bid her farewell.

Pedro had the children reform the circle around him. As he said his farewell, he waved his hand over his head and suddenly in front of each child there appeared a small rainbow. In front of Pedro was a huge rainbow through which everyone could see a large meadow filled with horses. Pedro urged his horse forward and he slowly rode through the arch of the rainbow into the meadow with the other horses. From the other side of the rainbow Pedro dismounted from the saddle, turned and waved. The children waved back and instantly the rainbow and Pedro disappeared.

From her rainbow, Mindy could see the cottage. As she looked through the other rainbows near her she could see a country home with mountains in one, a large apartment building in another and a farmyard in yet another. When they looked through their individual rainbows each child could see their way home. One by one the children passed through their rainbows. When each of them turned and waved goodbye, they instantly disappeared.

In no time at all, it seemed Mindy was the only guest left. She realized that as much as she hated to do so, it was her turn to go home. She took one last look around and reluctantly headed through the arch of the rainbow toward the cottage. The instant she turned and waved goodbye to Princess Min, her rainbow disappeared.

Pedro

Chapter 11

Mindy found herself standing in the exact same spot where she'd been standing when she first crossed into the land of Zot. The book she'd been carrying when Bolo instructed her to take the rainbow stick was still lying there on the ground, exactly where she'd placed it.

The first thing she noticed was that the sun was no longer shining. In fact, it was exactly the opposite. The sky above her was thick with clouds and it had grown very windy. At first it began raining very lightly, but within moments it turned into a heavy downpour.

Mindy quickly scooped up her book from the ground, ran to the cottage and scrambled onto the covered front deck.

"Did you get wet?" asked her Mom.

"A little," she replied.

"I was wondering when you'd finally come out of the rain. I thought I was going to have to come and get you."

"No," said Mindy. "In the land of Zot, the sun was shining and it was a beautiful day."

"Whatever are you talking about?" asked her Mom.

"Don't you remember Mom?" "I went to the party at Princess Min's castle."

"Oh right," sighed her mom. "I forgot again."

And so it was Mindy began describing her adventure in the land of Zot. She told them the whole story about Bolo, the rainbow, Princess Min, the carriage, all about the children, the magic of Pedro and so on. One by one the adults listened to her detailed account of the party. When she told them about her special powers, they all agreed she did have a wonderful imagination, but she also noticed as she told the story they were once again quietly smiling to themselves.

Even though they argued she'd only been gone a very short period of time, Mindy kept insisting she'd really been on an incredible journey.

"Here, look!" she exclaimed. "I've a rainbow bracelet and a picture stone to prove it!"

She held out her right arm to show off the bracelet, but it was nowhere to be seen. In a panic, she reached into her pocket but her picture stone was also missing. The only two things that could prove her visit to the land of Zot had both disappeared. Mindy knew the adults didn't believe her and now, she had no way to prove she'd been anywhere.

The remainder of her day was spent feeling discouraged. She didn't feel like talking any more so she sat by herself reading one of her books. At suppertime she again sat quietly at the table, afraid to bring up the subject for fear the adults would again tell her she'd only fallen asleep and had a little dream. "Maybe they are right," she said to herself. "Maybe I just fell asleep and had a dream."

That evening, as she was preparing for bed, Mindy went to the bathroom to brush her teeth. When she looked into the mirror, she remembered the words of Princess Min.

"Every time we look in the mirror we'll think of each other."

Standing there looking at herself in the mirror, she noticed the rainbow bracelet appeared to be on her right wrist. She immediately looked directly at her wrist but the bracelet was not there.

"How can it be," she said to herself. "When I look in the mirror, I'm wearing the bracelet, but when I'm not looking in the mirror the bracelet isn't here. This can't be real."

Her first instinct was to call her mom, but she needed some time to think it all through. As much as she wanted to think about it though, she was just too tired. It had been a very long day. For certain she didn't understand what she was seeing, but she was so tired she knew that more than anything she just had to sleep.

Electing to give it more thought tomorrow, she slowly made her way to her room, climbed into bed and crawled under the covers. During the process of moving about to get comfortable, she stuck her right hand under her pillow and noticed there was something under it. Slowly, she lifted the pillow and felt around in the dark to see what was there.

At first she thought it was a plastic toy or perhaps some doll accessories. Whatever it was, it was smooth and cold. She picked it up and held it in her right hand. It felt a lot like a stone. Although she couldn't see the object clearly in the darkness of the room, she transferred it into her left hand, shut her eyes and closed her palm. Instantly, the pictures began. There in beautiful color, the land of Zot unfolded before her. She didn't understand how or why, but the picture stone had appeared under her pillow.

Her immediate reaction was to take the stone to her parents and show them the proof of her journey. On the other hand, she remembered Bolo telling her the stone was created especially for her and wouldn't work for anyone else. Even if she told everyone this was her picture stone, they would probably think it was just another stone she found to add to her rock collection. No matter how many times she went over it in her mind, she always reached the same conclusion. It would be impossible to convince anyone the stone had magical powers.

As it ultimately turned out, the only thing that really mattered was whenever she placed the stone in her left hand and closed her eyes, the stone always rewarded her with its magic.

From that day forth, Mindy Magee faithfully carried her picture stone wherever she went. Whenever she told the story and anyone commented on her vivid imagination, she would just smile to herself and pat the stone in her pocket. After all, what did they really know about imagination? She was the one gifted with the special power.

About the Author

Dave Hepworth retired from the Royal Canadian Mounted Police in 2003 after a career spanning more than 38 years of service. Although the early years of Dave's career were spent as a police officer, he served more than 30 years as a Lab Specialist stationed at the RCMP Forensic Laboratory Service in Regina, Saskatchewan Canada. During his laboratory career, Dave routinely searched, identified and evaluated trace evidence from exhibit materials submitted to the Laboratory Service from crime scenes.

Throughout his life, Dave has pretty much seen it all. His career has given him great insight into the trials and tribulations of crime victims as well as the criminal mindset. It has also given him an acute awareness of the importance of properly nurturing our children to promote peace, understanding and goodwill throughout the world.

Dave was born and raised in a small rural town in southwestern Ontario Canada. He grew up in an era when there were few, if any TV sets available. For the most part, children entertained themselves by exercising their own imaginations.

In Dave's family, children's bedtime stories were often generated on the spot by parents and grandparents rather than read from books. Dave has kept that same story telling tradition with his own grandchildren and was inspired to write this book for his eldest grandchild who mastered the art of reading at a very early age.

The Picture Stone is Dave's first published novel. His previously published literary works have consisted largely of scientific papers. Will there be additional novels to follow? Well, let's just point out that Dave and his wife Kathy have four grandchildren.

Contact Author: dghepworth@sasktel.net

ISBN 141209053-9

9 781412 090537